W9-AAZ-138

SPACE MICE

Lori Haskins Houran

illustrated by Priscilla Alpaugh

Albert Whitman & Company • Chicago, Illinois

Two hungry mice.

Rumble. Rumble.

Not enough cheese.

Grumble. Grumble.

Holy moly.
Look at *this*!

A GIANT YELLOW
BALL OF SWISS!

Jot and scribble.

Plot and sketch.

Run to the hardware
store and fetch—

Hammer, pliers,
    wrench and socket.

All the stuff
to build a rocket!

Drill, bang, measure.

Saw and screw.

Paint and polish.

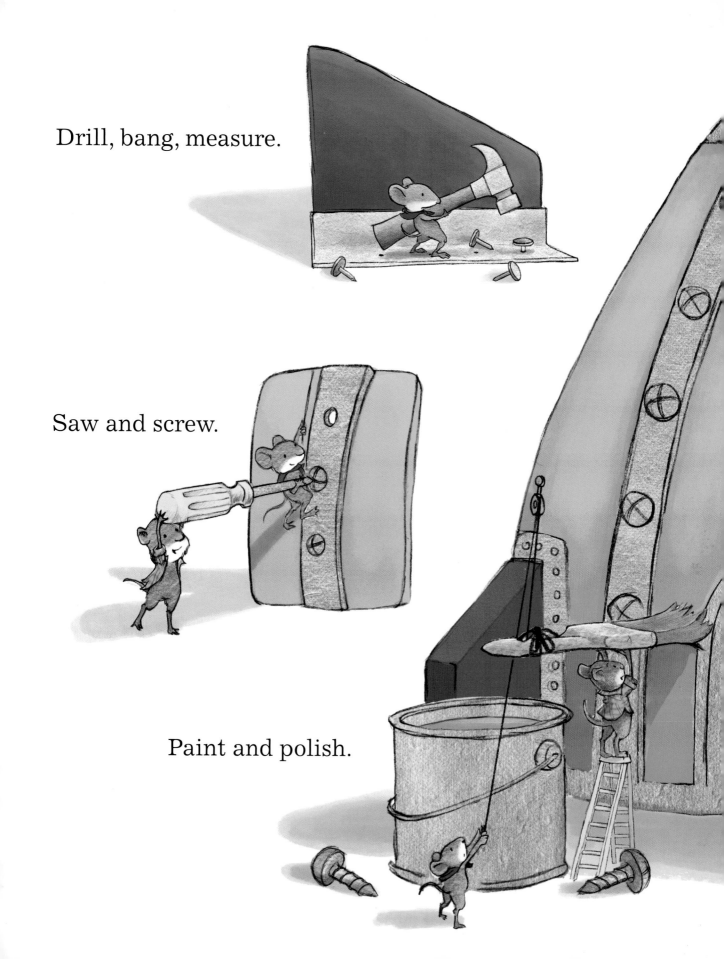

Suits on,
   boots on.

Mice on a mission.

Snap in, strap in.

Start the ignition!

A-OK!

Lift-off.

Countdown.

Space mice up
and on their way!

Landing, standing
on the moon.

That's one small step—

and one big spoon!

Nosh, munch, nibble.
Chomp and chew.
Stuff and swallow.

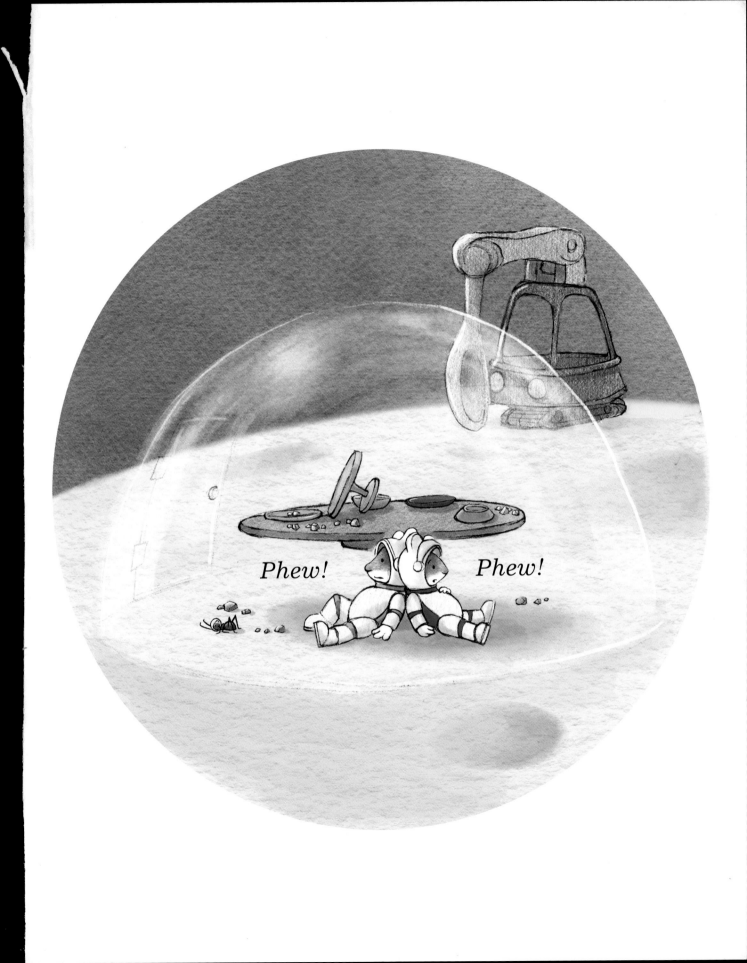

Back to the rocket.

(Take a slice!)

No full moon...

Just two full mice!

For Sanford, my cheddar half—LHH

For Julia, Marlo, and Emily. Team Weekly
Daily makes all things possible.—PA

Library of Congress Cataloging-in-Publication
data is on file with the publisher.

Text copyright © 2020 by Lori Haskins Houran
Illustrations copyright © 2020 by Priscilla Alpaugh
First published in the United States of America
in 2020 by Albert Whitman & Company

ISBN 978-0-8075-7553-6 (hardcover)
ISBN 978-0-8075-7566-6 (ebook)

All rights reserved. No part of this book may be reproduced
or transmitted in any form or by any means, electronic or
mechanical, including photocopying, recording, or by any
information storage and retrieval system, without permission
in writing from the publisher.

Printed in China
10 9 8 7 6 5 4 3 2 1 WKT 24 23 22 21 20 19

Design by Aphelandra Messer

For more information about Albert Whitman & Company,
visit our website at www.albertwhitman.com.